A Fish Named
YUM

MR. PIN, Vol. IV

by Mary Elise Monsell
illustrated by Eileen Christelow

ATHENEUM 1994 NEW YORK
Maxwell Macmillan Canada
Toronto
Maxwell Macmillan International
New York Oxford Singapore Sydney

Atheneum
Macmillan Publishing Company
866 Third Avenue
New York, NY 10022

Maxwell Macmillan Canada, Inc.
1200 Eglinton Avenue East
Suite 200
Don Mills, Ontario M3C 3N1

Macmillan Publishing Company is part of the
Maxwell Communication Group of Companies.

First edition
Printed in the United States of America
10 9 8 7 6 5 4 3 2 1

The text of this book is set in 12-point Century Old Style.

Library of Congress Cataloging-in-Publication Data
Monsell, Mary Elise.
A fish named Yum: Mr. Pin, vol. IV / by Mary Elise Monsell; illustrated by
Eileen Christelow. —1st ed.
p. cm.
Summary: Mr. Pin, the rockhopper penguin detective in Chicago, investigates
two cases involving a flood and a sinister fishnapping.
ISBN 0–689–31882–0
[1. Penguins—Fiction. 2. Chicago (Ill.)—Fiction. 3. Mystery and detective
stories.] I. Christelow, Eileen, ill. II. Title. III. Title: Mr. Pin.
PZ7.M7626Mt   1994
[Fic]—dc20   93–25731

With fond wishes to the very best of critics:
Taylor Shire. You are a special young lady.

With much appreciation from Mr. Pin to
John LaPlante, who loves Chicago and works
well with chocolate. Not easy to find that
kind of talent.

Many thanks to Mrs. Mandell's 1993
fifth-grade class.

Contents

The Great
Chicago Flood

1

Monday was quiet in Smiling Sally's Diner. But not for long. Mr. Pin had just polished off a stack of caramel fudge pancakes, leaving out the fudge. Mr. Pin had gained some weight since his arrival in Chicago. He had decided to cut back until he could see his feet—webbed feet, that is.

Mr. Pin was a rockhopper penguin, mostly black and white with long yellow plumes on both sides of his head. Some time ago, he had left the South Pole to be a detective in Chicago. After gangsters tried to blow up Smiling Sally's Diner, Mr. Pin moved into the room next to the kitchen. It would be soon enough when crime came by the diner again.

But back to Monday.

Sally was in the kitchen experimenting with chocolate chip cookies. Meanwhile, hiding from the smell of chocolate, Mr. Pin was in the basement conducting his own experiments. He was measuring the growth of his prized collection of philodendron plants.

Above his underground plant laboratory huge grow lights dangled from pipes and heating ducts. All around were sacks of potting soil, shovels, and organic spider mite spray. Next to the plant supplies lay sacks of flour and instant chocolate pudding mix piled chest high. Sally wanted Mr. Pin to help her get rid of it. She had bought it from Pete, the chicken man, and the pudding tasted awful. But Mr. Pin couldn't quite bring himself to throw out chocolate, even bad chocolate. Besides, every now and then truckers borrowed some of it to fill potholes in the alley.

Mr. Pin inserted a water sensor into the soil of a clay pot.

Hisssss-spurt! Strange sound, thought Mr. Pin. Was it a gas leak? Detecting no telltale smell, Mr. Pin looked for other clues. Then his feet started to get wet. Looking at the floor he realized the horrible truth. Smiling Sally's Diner had sprung a leak!

Ever alert, Mr. Pin studied the situation. This was no ordinary leak. Water spouted like Buckingham Fountain through a crack in the floor. The crack widened and a small fish popped out. Thinking fast, Mr. Pin picked up the fish by its flopping tail and

dropped it into a mason jar. He filled the jar with clean plant water.

Meanwhile, the leak was beginning to grow. It grew larger and larger, swelling into a small river zigzagging through the flour sacks. Mr. Pin moved some of the sacks on top of the crack, hoping to stop the flow. For now, things were under control. . . . Until all of a sudden, things got worse. Much worse. The grow lights went out! His plants were in total darkness!

2

Without light his plants were in grave danger. But an even greater danger lurked beneath the concrete floor.

Mr. Pin tucked the mason jar—with the fish swimming in tight circles—under his wing and went up to the diner. He put the fish on the counter and picked up the phone. His first call was to Herb's Bionic Garden. His second call was to Shedd Aquarium. The third call was to a plumber. After that, the phone went dead.

"What's going on?" asked Maggie. She was Sally's niece who lived upstairs and often helped Mr. Pin with his cases. "The phone's dead and my CB radio is out to lunch. Who's the fish?"

"Doesn't have a name yet," said Mr. Pin.

Sally came out of the kitchen looking worried.

7

"My cookies are half-baked," she said.

"Hardly," said Mr. Pin.

"So where'd you find the fish?" asked Maggie.

"In the basement."

"What bait did you use?" asked Maggie, believing almost anything was possible with Mr. Pin—even fishing in the basement.

"I don't know. Probably chocolate pudding. Actually," said Mr. Pin, "it popped through the floor when the leak started."

"What leak?" asked Sally.

"It's more like a flood."

"Flood?"

"In the basement," said Mr. Pin.

"Is that why we don't have electricity?" asked Sally. "Nothing works in my kitchen," she said looking directly at Mr. Pin. "And if the freezers don't work, the ice cream might melt."

"Terrible," said Mr. Pin raising his plumes.

"We have another problem too," said Maggie.

"What's that?" asked Mr. Pin.

"That fish is getting dizzy."

Just then a very tall white-haired man with spectacles walked into the diner carrying a wheel from his bicycle. Sally looked at the man then said, "I'm going to look for a bigger home for that fish."

"You must be Herb," Mr. Pin said to the man with the wheel.

"No, not Herb. Phil. Phil O. Dendrum," said the white-haired man.

"A plant expert," said Mr. Pin hopefully.

"Afraid not," said Phil.

"Then you're here about the fish," said Mr. Pin.

"No, I'm here about the flood."

"A plumber?" asked Mr. Pin.

"Not quite," said Phil. "Actually, I've heard all about you, Mr. Pin and I need *your* help."

"Really!" said Maggie.

Mr. Pin hopped up onto a diner stool and met Phil's concerned gaze.

"Chicago is flooding," said Phil. "Someone was drilling wood pilings into the Chicago River bed. An old freight tunnel that runs under the river and throughout the city was punctured. It's letting in the whole river. Now *everyone's* basement is flooding. Desks, chairs, books, papers, clothes, and fish are floating in several feet of water."

"Terrible!" said Maggie, her eyes growing wider.

"The electricity has been turned off so no one can be electrocuted," Phil went on. "Everyone downtown in the Loop has been sent home. Trains are overloaded. There's mass confusion."

"Sounds like a disaster," said Maggie.

"The worst," said Phil. "Probably since the Chicago fire."

"What can we do to help?" asked Mr. Pin.

"At the moment, I just want to find out how to plug the hole. I want to help the city. That's my job . . . helping the city, that is," said Phil. "In any case, that *used* to be my job."

"What do you mean *used* to be your job?" asked Mr. Pin.

Phil took off his round glasses, rubbed a crease between his eyes, then said: "I've been fired."

"Fired!" shouted Maggie angrily.

"I don't know why," said Phil. "I'm not even in charge of tunnels. But someone thought I was. *My* job is taking care of bridges, including the one above the leak. The terrible thing is I can't get near the place to help," said Phil.

"Now," said Mr. Pin quietly. "It appears there are two cases to solve. We have to stop the flood. Then, of course, we have to get Phil's job back."

"Shouldn't be too hard," said Maggie, looking at Mr. Pin hopefully.

Sally came out of the kitchen carrying a large glass cookie jar with the word YUM painted in bold green letters across the front.

"Only a few more hours before the ice cream will melt," she said, pouring the water and the fish into the larger jar.

"But at least," said Mr. Pin, "we have saved a fish."

3

Maggie wasn't sure a fish could look worried. But what fish would want to be in a glass cookie jar with the word YUM on the outside? Not only that, people were starting to *call* him Yum.

Sally looked worried too as Phil left with his bicycle wheel.

Maggie helped her make salami sandwiches while Mr. Pin paced back and forth, thinking.

"I hate to see all of this food go to waste," said Sally.

"Could you sell it?" asked Maggie.

"Maybe. But the ice cream will be ruined anyway."

"Ruined," said Mr. Pin. He thought for a moment then said, "What about a freezer truck?"

"Sounds like a good idea," said Maggie. "But

where will you find a freezer truck on a day like this?"

"How's your CB working?" asked Mr. Pin.

"Could be better. It needs electricity. Why?"

"There's another one in the basement."

"Right, but it needs batteries ... batteries! Of course. I bet I could get it to work. Then what?"

"Put the word out to the truckers that you need a freezer truck fast. Tell them it's an emergency. Something to do with ice cream, especially chocolate. They'll understand if they know it's for Smiling Sally's."

But there wasn't much time to talk. Saving ice cream and fixing radios would have to wait until after lunch.

Smiling Sally's filled quickly when people discovered it was still open. Dozens of hungry flood workers carried helmets under their arms as they stomped into the diner with their heavy rubber boots. There were even some workers outfitted in diving equipment. It was beginning to look like the set for the "Undersea World of Jacques Cousteau." One of the divers left a small pump for Sally which would keep the diner, for a little while, above sea level.

After clearing away a mountain of dishes that couldn't be washed, Maggie went upstairs to see if she could get a portable CB radio to work. Sally gave away the leftover food to a homeless shelter then decided to walk to a camping store to find a Coleman stove. That left Mr. Pin with the job of saving his plants from total darkness and the city from too much water.

4

In the eerie reaches of Smiling Sally's basement, Mr. Pin was well-equipped. A large flashlight was tucked under his wing along with rope, rubber waders, and a pump. He looked like he was ready for fly-fishing in a swollen stream.

The flies would have to wait. In the flashlight's beam, Mr. Pin saw that the floor was wet, but the water wasn't too deep. Not yet anyway. Mr. Pin left the rubber waders on the stairs then took the long hose of the water pump and directed it to where most of the water appeared to be coming in.

Then Mr. Pin surveyed the rest of the basement. The flour sacks he'd placed on the crack were just about ruined, but the rest of the diner's supplies would be all right for a little while, since they were stacked on shelves.

His plants were another story. How long, he wondered, could they survive in the dark under these swamplike conditions? Pump or no pump, the water might rush in and flood the whole basement. The risk was great.

The plants had to go. One by one, Mr. Pin ferried the heavy pots across the rising water and hauled them upstairs into the diner. By late afternoon, Smiling Sally's looked like Herb's Bionic Garden.

Mr. Pin was just taking his last plant up the basement stairs when he heard a voice booming through the back door.

"Where would you like the truck?"

"Not in here," said Mr. Pin completely hidden behind the plant.

Hank, the trucker, jumped about three feet in the air. Then he parted the vines. He looked at the plant more closely.

"Mr. Pin!" he said seeing the rockhopper. "Uh, sorry, I thought it was a talking plant."

"Afraid not," said Mr. Pin. "I only talk *to* my plants."

Getting over the shock, Hank said: "I heard you need a freezer truck."

"Absolutely!" said Mr. Pin as he put the plant on the counter. "Chocolate ice cream is in danger."

"Danger?"

"Right. You never know when you're going to need a few gallons of chocolate ice cream."

16

"Of course," said Hank.

With renewed energy, Hank and Mr. Pin hauled Sally's softening ice cream outside to the alley where a freezer truck was parked. Hank offered to bring another truck if it would help keep the diner business going.

The diner was quiet when Hank finally left. Surrounded by plants, Mr. Pin took a moment to rest his feet. He sat back in a booth and pretty soon his beak fell onto his chest. He wasn't asleep long before he heard an unusual announcement:

"Mr. Pin! Fish are swimming under City Hall."

"Krill are swimming in the Arctic," Mr. Pin answered in his sleep. Then he rubbed his eyes with his wings and looked at the towering figure of Phil O. Dendrum, his white hair rising just above Mr. Pin's indoor garden.

"Are you sure you're not a plant expert?" the sleepy penguin asked before recognizing the man who needed his help.

"Not this kind of plant," said Phil. "But we have a real problem. The newspapers say that workers have thrown mattresses and concrete blocks on the hole in the riverbed. I wish I could do something. No one seems to be able to plug it for good. Not only that, it's beginning to rain."

"There has to be something that will work," said Mr. Pin.

"There have been many suggestions," said Phil. "Some of them are a little unusual."

"Such as?"

"Landfill garbage," said Phil.

"Not a bad idea. There is a lot of it. But some of it would float, and it might get smelly."

"How about peanut butter?"

"Excellent to eat but not to plug holes," said Mr. Pin. "There's always chewing gum. It would be disastrous, of course, if I ever tried to chew any."

"I understand," said Phil. "How about newspapers?"

"Or government memos," said Mr. Pin.

"Old shoes."

"Jell-O."

"Too soft."

"Gerbil shavings. Maggie has plenty of them."

"How about an old-fashioned beaver dam?" suggested Phil.

They were beginning to sound desperate.

"Good idea," said Mr. Pin. But where would they find a crew of willing beavers at this late hour, not to mention all the trees they'd need.

Sitting in the back room of Smiling Sally's Diner, Mr. Pin and Phil worked late into the night. Sally brought them a thermos of hot chocolate and Maggie came in every now and then to offer a few more suggestions. They talked until almost midnight. Then Mr. Pin heard sounds he would not want to hear again:

Crack! Hissssss! Whoooosh!

It sounded like the diner was blowing apart.

5

Fearing the worst, Mr. Pin and Phil hurried to the basement stairs. This time Mr. Pin started to put on the rubber waders, then thought better of the idea when he tried to get them over his webbed feet. He left them hanging on the basement door.

One step at a time, he went down the dark, creaking stairs while Phil stayed at the top. Mr. Pin was all alone with whatever it was, deep in the dark basement. Before reaching the bottom of the stairs, he felt the water already climbing up his feet. Easily hopping into the water, he swam through the basement to the site of the leak. It was gushing water now! The terrifying noise must have been caused by the water widening the crack in the concrete floor.

Mr. Pin thought fast. He thought about all of the

things he and Phil suggested to stop the city's flood. He thought about Jell-O. Then he thought about something else. There it was, just out of reach, the answer to all of his problems.

Mr. Pin swam through the rising water. Maggie, who had come down from her apartment when she heard the explosion of water, stood next to Phil at the top of the stairs. She directed a flashlight at Mr. Pin.

"What's he doing?" asked Maggie.

"I don't know," said Phil. "I can't see."

Snargle. Glurgle. Sput!

Maggie looked at Phil. "Something strange is going on down there," she said, handing the flashlight to Phil.

"All I can see is something that looks like a slowly moving glacier," said Phil.

Splurgle. Glug. Rrrrrrosh!

"What's that?" asked Maggie.

Then they heard Mr. Pin ponderously make his way back up the basement stairs.

Exhausted, the penguin padded into the diner, his feathers matted together. He held his side with a wet wing and lowered himself into a booth.

"Too bad about the waders," he said. "Might have come in handy." He looked annoyed.

"What's wrong?" asked Phil who was concerned.

"The leak was fixed. But the price was . . . high." Mr. Pin couldn't bring himself to say any more.

22

6

Phil wasn't sure what really happened in Sally's basement. He was hoping he'd find out. But he knew he'd have to wait. When he dropped by the diner the next morning, Mr. Pin had a plan.

"You're going to have a chance to help the city," said Mr. Pin.

"We're going to plug the river?" asked Phil.

"Exactly. But first, you're going to need a disguise," he told Phil.

"Of course," said Phil. "I could always be a plant expert."

"And I'm going to need a long rope, fishing buckets, and several trucks."

"How many trucks?" asked Maggie.

"As many as you can get," replied Mr. Pin.

"No problem," said Maggie, thinking of Hank.

Phil looked surprised, but then again everything that happened in the diner was surprising. After a moment, he offered to bring the fishing buckets.

"Good. I'll take care of everything else," said Mr. Pin. "We go to work at midnight."

Maggie was thinking that midnight was a good time to solve mysteries. But what did Mr. Pin mean by "everything else"? Knowing Mr. Pin, it could be almost anything. Maggie knew she would find out soon enough. There was plenty of work to do. Answers would come later.

Mr. Pin said he was going to Pete's Chocolate Emporium. Maggie went upstairs to talk on her CB. That left Phil to find fishing buckets and get into a disguise.

Later that night, Phil found Mr. Pin asleep again, this time on the counter—wings on his chest and feet straight up in the air. He was surrounded by waterproof lights, rope, and an assortment of fishing supplies. Phil left him alone and curled up in a booth. There was time to rest before midnight and whatever Mr. Pin had planned. When Sally saw them both asleep some time later, she brought pillows and blankets, then blew out the candles they used for light.

They wouldn't be out long.

Around eleven o'clock, the quiet was suddenly

broken by the sound of a portable radio broadcasting an old baseball game. It was a tape Mr. Pin used as an alarm clock.

Runners are in the corners. The game is tied 5 to 5, top of the seventh.

Phil woke up slowly and put on his disguise: a fake beard, a helmet, and heavy work clothes. He decided to forget about the sunglasses. It wouldn't make any sense to be wearing them at midnight and might arouse suspicion. Then he looped a rope around his waist.

Mr. Pin wasn't looking much like himself either. He had put on goggles, a waterproof watch, and an underwater equipment belt. The ropes and fishing equipment were draped around his wide stomach.

Nice wing on that penguin, the radio broadcaster said.

"I remember that game," said Maggie, coming down the stairs. "You were great. The Case of the Spitter Pitchers. Are you sure you can walk around in that stuff?" Maggie had a way of talking all at once.

"This is the easy part," said Mr. Pin. "The rest could be dangerous."

Suddenly a truck roared down the alley. Hank burst through the back door. He said a "few" trucks were parked just outside.

"Very satisfactory," said Mr. Pin.

"What do you want us to do with the trucks?" asked Hank. "Rescue more ice cream?"

"Not this time. We're going to fix a leak. By the way, our first stop will be Pete's Chocolate Emporium on the west side."

Maggie wasn't sure what Pete's had to do with the flood. Pete, also known as the chicken man, had bought the factory to manufacture chocolate pigeons for his chicken shop. But that was another story. Sally and Mr. Pin usually bought most of their chocolate from Luigi the pasta man. Some things made no sense.

It was a strange group that rode west into the eerie, blacked-out midnight city. Under Mr. Pin's direction, a caravan of sixty-five trucks followed the detective to Pete's factory and then to the Kinzie Street Bridge, which overlooked the leaking river.

It was an even stranger sight when a disguised Phil convinced workers to allow a rockhopper penguin to inspect the damage.

The air was brisk. A crowd gathered and people held their breath as Mr. Pin dived into a dangerously swirling eddy to examine the leak. The water was too murky for a light to be of any help. But Mr. Pin could feel the water being sucked out of the river into the tunnel that flooded the city's underbelly. At any moment, the current could pull Mr. Pin into the tunnel. Phil was getting worried.

"It's too dangerous," he said to a worker. "Get the divers."

But before they could get their equipment on, Mr. Pin finally came up and gave the command:

"Bring the buckets!"

Maggie stood by, ready for anything. But she wasn't sure she'd ever be ready for this. One bucket at a time, Mr. Pin pulled buckets with flopping fish out of the narrow hole where they were trapped. Then they were loaded into a larger tank on one of the trucks.

Phil gave the signal:

"Unload the trucks!"

At first, Phil wasn't sure what would come out of those trucks. But suddenly it all made sense.

Never would the Chicago River look like this again. The truckers formed a line from their trucks and passed bucket after bucket of instant chocolate pudding mix fresh from Pete's Chocolate Emporium. It didn't taste very good. But it was great for fixing floods. Better than fast drying concrete. In less than an hour the eddying whirlpool had stopped. The hole was plugged. The danger was over.

"So *that's* what you used to fix the leak in the diner," said Phil.

"A good way to get rid of bad chocolate," said Mr. Pin.

Television crews and newspaper reporters hurried over to find out how the flood had been stopped so quickly when so many had tried and failed.

"Sorry," said Mr. Pin, "no more pictures. But you can talk to Phil. A great man who loves this city and never should have been fired. Not only that, he works well with chocolate. Not easy to find that kind of talent."

Mr. Pin took the long way back to Smiling Sally's Diner. He needed time to think things over. As he walked along Michigan Avenue, he watched the sun come up over the Art Institute, a friendly sight after seeing too much water.

Caramel fudge pancakes were on his mind. A good stack with extra chocolate syrup. Besides, with all the work he had done, he was able to see his feet again.

Settling in with Smiling Sally's best pancakes, Mr. Pin unfolded the morning paper to the front page. There was a large picture of him holding buckets of fish. Next to that was a picture of Phil with a head-line Mr. Pin would probably put in his memoirs:

PHIL O. DENDRUM—A GREAT MAN WHO
WORKS WELL WITH CHOCOLATE!

Nice to be quoted. Nice to hear that about Phil. But even better, with that praise, he might get his job back. At least the city might recognize a true hero. Besides, he had even managed to save a few fish. Not a bad day's work.

It was just about time to get back to writing his memoirs and watering his plants ... his plants! He'd almost forgotten.

Just then, the door opened slowly. A man who could have been Phil's twin stepped into the diner. A shock of white hair caught the sun as he came inside.

"We'll be open in a few minutes," said Mr. Pin. "Can I help you?"

"Why, yes, I think so, uh, I don't know," he said. "I need to talk to a Mr. Pin. My Name is Dr. Herbert Rootrot from Herb's Bionic Garden. I'm a plant expert."

A Fish Named Yum

1

Chicago was hit hard by a blizzard that had frozen pipes and closed schools. Buses ran late. Snowplows buried cabs. And more snow was on the way.

It was a bad day to be out. But it was a good day to be inside Smiling Sally's Diner on Monroe. Mr. Pin was helping Sally bake chocolate chip cookies. He tasted every batch that came out of the oven. Along with her cinnamon rolls, the cookies were beginning to make Sally famous.

In fact, Sally's cookies were so good that truckers took bags of them on long trips. The word about Sally's cookies was spreading fast. A businesswoman said Sally should sell them to stores and call them "Famous Shamus" cookies after Mr. Pin.

"It's a good idea, except who would know that a *shamus* is a detective," Sally had said. "But I'll think about it."

Besides eating, Mr. Pin spent much of the morning hand-feeding chocolate chips to his fish named Yum. Since the fish had popped out of the basement during the great Chicago flood, the diner had become his home. There was only one problem. Yum was a picky eater. He refused to eat regular fish food. He ate only the chocolate chips Mr. Pin hand-fed him. Not only that, they had to be fresh chips from Luigi's Pasta Shop. Luigi sold only the best pasta and chocolate. Mr. Pin knew that. And Yum knew that. They had something of . . . an understanding.

So at the height of the blizzard, when Yum ran out of sustaining food and Sally ran out of her secret ingredient, there was only one thing to do. Mr. Pin headed into the storm.

It was a mission of chocolate. An appointment with destiny. A time when only the brave or the desperate faced the perils of Chicago's snowbound streets.

Mr. Pin fought the swirling, blinding snow several blocks down Monroe to Luigi's. Speed on dry land was not Mr. Pin's specialty. But he naturally loved the cold and made up some time by tobogganing down snowbanks . . . beak first.

While Mr. Pin revelled in the snow, a shadowy figure in a trenchcoat lurked in the doorway of a sushi shop. Unseen by the rockhopper penguin, he watched Mr. Pin slide down Monroe. Then he slipped into the diner.

In addition to slow overland speed, Mr. Pin was not noted for his speed in chocolate shops. It was several diet-free hours later when Mr. Pin returned to the diner from Luigi's. He was barely recognizable. His checked cap and red muffler were completely white. Salt from the streets stung his webbed feet, and his yellow plumes were iced together. But the dangerous mission was a success. Tucked under his wing was a large sack of chocolate chips.

"There's been trouble," said Sally.

"Trouble," said Mr. Pin setting the bag on the counter. "Looks like I returned just in time."

"It's Yum," said Maggie.

"Why yes, the chocolate is quite tasty," said Mr. Pin.

"Not the chips," said Maggie, "the fish."

"Yum!" said Mr. Pin, unwinding his red muffler.

"He's gone," said Sally.

"Gone?" asked Mr. Pin, slowly creating a large puddle of melting snow.

"Yum," said Sally, "has been fishnapped!"

2

L ate that afternoon, it was a small gathering of mournful diners who discussed Yum's disappearance over mugs of hot chocolate. The truckers were fond of the fish that had grown rapidly under Mr. Pin's watchful eye and generous wing. The resident detective, himself, sat somewhat apart considering the case. Every now and then he would shake his head and say something like, "I can't believe it," or "Impossible. Doesn't make sense."

But there it was. The fish Mr. Pin had befriended and taught to love chocolate was now missing. Not only that, it was possible that Yum had fallen into desperate hands.

Mr. Pin reviewed the facts. Yum had been fishnapped while Mr. Pin was out buying chocolate. Sally and Maggie were in the kitchen making cookies. The diner was empty. It would have been all too easy for the thief to make his move then.

There were plenty of footprints on the black and white tile floor. Which ones belonged to Yum's fishnapper? A fish doesn't just walk away. One of the truckers *had* seen a short, shadowy figure lurking in the doorway of a nearby sushi shop just that morning. But what diabolical mind would steal a fish in the middle of one of Chicago's worst snowstorms?

There was a possibility he didn't want to consider. Gargoyle! Master spy. Had Gargoyle, the Spy Who Came North from the Pole, returned to Chicago to cause greater chaos? And for what reason? And why would he steal a fish?

The police were hesitant to help.

"We'll keep an eye out," Sergeant O'Malley had said on the phone. "We don't have to wait twenty-four hours to say he's missing. But in any case, unless Yum's a person, we can't file a report. Sorry."

"No harm in checking," Mr. Pin had said.

His thoughts now were interrupted by the ring of Sally's pay phone.

"It's for you," said Hank, handing the phone to Mr. Pin. The detective pulled the long cord out of the booth and leaned against the accordion door.

The connection rattled with the strange sound of some kind of motor in the background.

"All right, Pin, here's the story." It was a low gravelly voice, probably disguised.

Mr. Pin held up his wing to silence the diner.

"Can't get something for nothing," said the strange voice.

"What is it you have?" asked Mr. Pin coolly.

"Just listen," said the voice.

Mr. Pin tipped his head and held the phone close. It was the sound of a pump . . . just like the kind used in a fish tank!

"Is he all right?" asked Mr. Pin.

"For now," said the voice. "I'll be in touch. Meanwhile, be prepared to pay more than a fin for your fish!"

Click.

Mr. Pin knew he was right about one thing. A fish and his chips are soon parted. Yum had fallen into desperate hands.

3

"Now what?" asked Maggie later that night. "Yum is gone. The police won't help. And whoever stole our fish probably wants more money than we have."

Mr. Pin was quiet for a moment. Perhaps he had missed something. Something right under his beak. Maybe even in the diner itself. The fishnapper was likely to call again. In the meantime, Mr. Pin had to do something.

"We need to look for clues," said Mr. Pin.

"In the diner?" asked Maggie.

"Exactly."

Mr. Pin hopped off his typing crate in the back room, which he called both home and office, and headed for the darkened diner. He brought along his black bag. Sally had closed the diner early and gone upstairs to pay a few bills. Maggie followed closely on the heels of Mr. Pin.

First he retraced the possible path of the fish-napper. From his black bag he took out a large magnifying glass. He had asked Sally not to clean the floor.

"Hmmm. There is something suspicious here. Something white and gluelike."

"Can't be snow," said Maggie. "What else is white?"

"I'm not sure," said Mr. Pin, slipping a sample into a plastic bag.

"What's that?" asked Maggie.

"Evidence," said Mr. Pin. He padded slowly from the door over to the diner stools. Sally had already cleaned the counter, but there was a chance she had missed something underneath.

"What are you looking for now?" asked Maggie.

"I won't know until I find it," said Mr. Pin.

"Makes sense," said Maggie.

"There!" shouted Mr. Pin. He had spotted it on the side of the old green marble counter right next to where Yum's jar once sat.

"Definitely chocolate," he said, extending his wing and preening. Then he announced: "This is very familiar."

"You could have tasted it in the diner, maybe it's just some smooshed chocolate chips," suggested Maggie.

"Not possible," said Mr. Pin. "This is not Luigi's chocolate. I am certain of that. It is quite tasty, but not as good as Luigi's."

"It's amazing," said Maggie. "Everything's chocolate. Chocolate dinosaur eggs. Chocolate pudding. Chocolate pigeons. Chocolate ice cream. And then there was the time we went to bakeries, dozens of them, all over Chicago to sample chocolate."

"Crimes of chocolate," said Mr. Pin softly, "are what I know best." He started to pace back and forth, musing about the small sample of chocolate still clinging to his wing.

Somewhere he had tasted this chocolate before. But where? It was a little late to visit bakeries. And what would that prove? Mr. Pin remembered his stomachache after solving the Case of the Picasso Thief. Too much chocolate seemed to be a hazard of the business.

There was another thing to keep in mind: the short, shadowy figure near the diner. He didn't want to admit it, but the evidence was there. Could it really be Gargoyle? That spy had slipped through his wings before. Would he do it again? He had been after a government codebook then. That's all Mr. Pin knew. What mission might he be on now? And why . . . would he steal a fish named Yum? Some gargoyles looked like fish. Was there a connection?

Some cases, thought Mr. Pin, were slippery indeed.

4

It had been almost twenty-four hours since Yum was fishnapped from the diner. Mr. Pin was worried. How long could his fish go without chocolate chips? Mr. Pin even had trouble eating his caramel fudge pancakes, one of Sally's specialties.

The diner had cleared out early. It was still snowing and a lot of people just stayed home. Maggie's school was closed so Mr. Pin had help thinking about Yum.

Brrrring! It was a cold sound in the warm diner coming from the phone booth in the corner. Mr. Pin picked up the phone as he wedged himself into the tiny booth.

"I got your fish," said a raspy voice. A tank gurgled in the background. Mr. Pin felt a lump in his throat.

"Who are you?" he asked with authority. He motioned for Maggie to come over and listen.

"Never mind that," growled the voice.

"Why do you want our fish?" asked Mr. Pin.

"You're the detective. Figure it out. *Bing.* Time's up. I'll make it easy for you. I want ransom."

"Ransom?" asked Mr. Pin startled. "We are hardly in a position to pay anything. None of us has any money."

"Too bad," snarled the fishnapper. "I want something better. You have a secret recipe that I need."

"Which one is that?" asked Mr. Pin.

"Okay. Here it is, penguin. I want a batch of Sally's chocolate chip cookies along with her recipe. And I want them by midnight tonight or your fish sizzles. Ha!"

Click.

What cruelty. What sinister, twisted criminal mind could put the life of an innocent fish in jeopardy.

"What did he want?" asked Maggie.

"It's worse than I thought," said Mr. Pin. "He wants Sally's chocolate chip cookies and her recipe or Yum will be a fish fry. And it's not even Friday."

"That's terrible," said Maggie.

"The fishnapper might be Gargoyle."

"How do you know?" asked Maggie.

50

"He's short," said Mr. Pin. "He probably likes chocolate, judging from the sample I found in the diner. He seems to like fish that look like gargoyles. And, of course, he'd steal a recipe that could make him millions for his spy operation."

"Oh, no," said Maggie. "We have to act fast."

"Right," said Mr. Pin.

"So how do we find Gargoyle?" asked Maggie.

"I don't know," said Mr. Pin. "But I'm beginning to get an idea."

The snow was getting much worse. It was piled up so high that customers couldn't see out the diner's windows. Every now and then, Mr. Pin went out to clear a path in the snow to the door. Some of the truckers were snowed in on Monroe and just stayed in the diner all day. It looked like they might even spend the night in sleeping bags. No one was going anywhere.

Except for Mr. Pin. He suddenly remembered where he had tasted that chocolate before.

"We need to get to Ohio Street," he announced.

"Have you thought about using the phone," drawled Sally, her hands on her hips. "It took you hours to go to Luigi's. Ohio is much farther."

"I have to visit a bakery."

"I think you've been working too hard," said Sally.

Maggie was worried. This had happened before. She wasn't sure Mr. Pin could stop with just one bakery.

Just then two frozen cross-country skiers stopped in for hot chocolate. Mr. Pin talked with them for a moment then turned to Maggie.

"You're on the ski team, aren't you?"

"Absolutely."

"Then perhaps you can help me put on these skis."

Maggie had seen stranger things since she had known Mr. Pin, but not too many. It wasn't easy fitting the bindings around Mr. Pin's webbed feet. She suggested boots, but he didn't react well to the idea. And she knew it was going to look a little strange to anyone else who might see them—a penguin and a red-haired girl—cross-country skiing down Michigan Avenue. It seemed like a lot of work just to visit a bakery.

But Mr. Pin had other things on his mind and not all of them involved chocolate.

Once outdoors, the two stayed aloft on the snow and made record time to the north end of the city. Few people were out except someone making a snowman and a few other skiers taking advantage of the snowed-in city. When Mr. Pin and Maggie turned down Ohio Street, they skied alone between mountainous peaks of snow. Just ahead, behind Chicago's snowy version of Pikes Peak, was a bakery.

"I remember this place," said Maggie. "But what could it possibly have to do with . . . "

"Flour," said Mr. Pin.

"Flour?" asked Maggie.

"The flour I found on the diner floor."

"But how do you know it belongs to this bakery?" asked Maggie, releasing her bindings then helping Mr. Pin with his.

"Do you remember another case where a famous painting was stolen?"

"The Picasso," said Maggie.

"Exactly. Anyway, the chocolate I found in the diner is the same chocolate the Picasso thief used in his bakery."

"I remember," said Maggie. "It was an unusual case."

"Right. But we have other fish to fry and I don't mean Yum."

"You mean Gargoyle?"

Mr. Pin didn't answer. He was already heading into the bakery dragging one pair of skis behind him. Maggie wasn't sure what he was going to do with the skis in the bakery, but she wanted to find out. She also wanted to finally meet Gargoyle, so she followed the detective inside.

The front room was empty. They could hear mixers in the back, along with what sounded like a gurgling tank. Maggie looked with concern at Mr. Pin who crept toward the kitchen behind the counter.

"You stay here," he ordered.

Maggie muttered something under her breath that sounded a lot like "right," then inched her way toward the kitchen.

Just before reaching the open doorway, Mr. Pin pulled an extralarge wedding cake out of a cooler. He placed it directly in front of the doorway then stepped around it into the windowless kitchen.

"I want my fish!" demanded Mr. Pin.

"You're not Gargoyle," said Maggie to a startled baker. He looked up from a cake he was decorating.

"A red herring," said Mr. Pin to Maggie.

Quickly, Mr. Pin turned out the lights. The baker made a dash for the front door, but Mr. Pin was ready. A carefully placed ski tripped the baker who plunged headfirst into one of his own cakes.

Mr. Pin turned the lights back on, dipped his wing into some of the chocolate from the cake, and announced:

"As I suspected. This is the same chocolate I found in the diner. And you are none other than the

Picasso thief. You must be out on parole. I see you have returned to a life of crime. Too bad, your cake is delicious."

"My cookies were going to be famous too," said the thief in the cake. "I needed that recipe to start a cookie business. The first time I tried those cookies, I knew I could be rich."

"Sally's cookies," said Mr. Pin. "Not yours."

Meanwhile, Maggie had found a phone and was calling the police who promised to get there by snowmobile. Could they hold the fishnapper until then?

"No problem," she said. "Mr. Pin's on the cake . . . on the case. I mean he's stuck in a cake . . . the thief, that is."

While Maggie was on the phone, Mr. Pin found a large tank containing several fish. It did not appear that the fishnapper was going to fry his fish after all. He liked fish. There was only one problem. All of the fish looked alike. Could one of them be Yum?

Ever ready for emergencies, Mr. Pin pulled a small paper bag out of the backpack he had worn. He carefully dropped a few chips into the tank. All of the fish ignored the chocolate. All but one. Familiar fins rose slowly, examined the chips, then ate hungrily. Yum had been found!